INTERVALLAQUA

The Gaps

Contents

Foreword

This is the Tenth book in my series of poetic wanderings through the obsessive world of Outlander the books, so wonderfully written by Diana Gabaldon. And the TV series so ably produced by Starz.

My work could be viewed as Fan Fiction or as I prefer to view it – an homage to the original work. I do not seek to re write the plot or redesign the characters. I do sometimes endeavour to 'get inside the mind' of the character and express a scene from a different perspective.

This book is a sweeping up operation. Having read the books several times and the series more often I suspect, I was still finding patches of text which I had not read properly, and which were deserving of more thorough attention.

I post my work on several face book groups and have the occasional request week where members can request a poem on any part of any book or any part of the show which they choose, and I will endeavour to write one for them.

This has generated more material and then requests for another book. And so on and so forth until here we are on book 10.

Again, I credit the amazing Lyn Fuller with the cover artwork.

I acknowledge and give credit to the masterful writing of Diana Gabaldon, and the amazing talent of the cast, crew and production team of the TV Series which we all hope will be in production until THE END.

Enough of me babbling on – read on and enjoy another poetic wander through the stones.

ALL REVENUE FROM MY WORK IS
DONATED TO RIDING FOR THE DISABLED.

This is a charity where I volunteer as a
Riding Coach, and which does marvellous
work with disabled children and adults
improving their physical ability, mental
health and wellbeing through the medium of
riding and horses.

The charity can only carry out its life
changing activities thanks to the generosity of
donors, the dedication of volunteers and the
good nature of the fantastic horses.

RDA It's what you can do that counts

Riding for the Disabled Association
Incorporating Carriage Driving

Through a looking glass darkly

War will change a person,
It is corrosion in your mind,
The blood, the screams, the terror,
They are never left behind.

We jollied on regardless,
Pretending life was new.
Re connecting with a past,
None of which was true.

Now I was professor's wife,
Frank had found his role.
History at Oxford,
Had always been his goal.

A woman now in limbo,
Searching for a life
Scarred by war, immersed in blood,
Could not just be a wife.

Would I settle easy,
Into domestic bliss,
Home and hearth and children,
I was not designed for this.

I brushed the tangles from my hair,
Each one was a thought,
I'd trained to use my talents,
Would all that count for nought.

A life without fulfilment
A life that's pre-defined
A life without adventure,
Is that for what I'd signed.

There is a crackle in the air,
A sense of things to come,
This night when ghosts can walk at large,
Will make my senses hum.

Lights go out to darkness,
Candles light the room,
And Frank believes he's seen a ghost,
Out there in the gloom.

Is it a subtle shift in time?
Alignment of the stars,
A life with less, but with far more,
Calls silent from afar.

Sub cruce candida
The white cross in my heart,
To tunes of Grey and Scarlett,
Marching to the past.

My conscience tried to call me,
My sense of duty strong,
I loved the man I married first,
How could that be wrong.

But as I sat and brushed my knots,
And cursed my curly hair,
My heart was stolen by a ghost,
I did not see him there.

The Call of Samhain

Mists of Autumn cloud the air,
It's dreich the locals say,
That wetting fog that damps your hair,
They know it's in to stay.

At dusk I wandered, lost and sad
Two hundred years had gone,
Time to find the one I love,
Time to journey on.

Restless warrior dressed in plaid,
A window bathed in light,
She brushes tangles from her hair,
With language impolite.

She cannot feel my presence yet,
Her mind a restless maze,
I watch her, and my spirit locks
Her soul under my gaze.

Two hundred years of purgatory,
To purge a life of sin,
Two hundred years without her light
My heart still holds hods her in.

Set free to walk this land once more,
Set free my mortal soul
I call her back into my time,
I only have one goal.

I call your body through the stones,
High upon that hill,
A power of mind, a strength of thought,
You can't deny my will.

Time for me is nothing,
For you I'm always here,
I've loved you always, from beyond
My vision always clear.

Come back to me, blood of my blood
Hear me, bone of my bone,
Don't be afraid, there's two of us,
We shall never be alone.

'Tis one night, in all the year,
I'm free at last to walk,
Come with me now my Sassenach,
I've not come here to talk.

Two hundred years without ye,
I've seen ye every day,
Felt your body close to me,
But not touched ye since that day,

Yer Bonnie hair, all wild and free,
Yer body made for mine,
I call ye now, come back to me
This night the stones align.

Reading the leaves

A worker's hand, but cared for,
Fingers long and deft,
The right is bare of ornament,
A gold ring on the left.

The lines are strong and well defined,
They show a course in life,
A break here overlapping,
She will be twice a wife.

The tea leaves showed a journey,
The man as yet unknown,
To travel far, but in a time,
Far distant from our own.

There is one explanation,
The one the stories tell,
The stones have sent her back in time,
Two hundred years the spell.

She will return, the travellers do,
But changed – not as they were,
Her palm says she will marry there,
The rest is still a blur,

Readings foretell many things,
They can but cast their net,
A palm is life as it unfolds,
It hasn't happened yet.

A stranger palm I never saw,
The leaves they contradict
A lifetime in a time gone by,
Is what they must predict.

Ambush

Cocknammon Rock – an Ambush?
Redcoats in the stones
Tulach Ard screamed in my ear,
Chilled me to my bones.

Thrown into the brambles,
Gorse prickles in my bum
Hideaway and ye 'll be safe
Wait until I come,

I must go back, must get away
I must get back to Frank,
At least I haven't been defiled,
I have these men to thank.

Gunshots, screaming, Clash of swords
Musket fire and smoke
I've not stayed where he threw me,
I have run, this is no joke

A desperate game of hide and seek
Hear hoofbeats on the ground,
Round the turn I see him plain
Oh, damn him, I've been found!

Bloodstained, sweating Breathing hard,
Dismounts warrior way,
If I run fast and dodge a bit
I might just get away

Blue eyes look me up and down,
Assessing, what to do
Drawn sword threatens certain death
But would he run me through

Ye know yer coming with me,
Before ye get much older,
Ye din'nae look too heavy lass,
I will throw ye o'er ma shoulder,

Something says he means it,
And it's holding some appeal,
I shake my head to clear the dream
But he is very real.

I find I am a hero,
The lads have had some fun
Whisky passed between them
They toast, a skirmish won

Take a swig now Sassenach
Twill help tae calm yer hunger
I can hear yer wame a rumbling
It sounds like distant thunder.

Please Mrs Fitz

Please can we keep her Mrs Fitz
Ye ken she's only wee
She's mainly hair and temper,
Can she no stay for tea,

We decided on the journey
She was nae a Whore,
And Murtagh says she's no a spy
And he's seen spies before

I'll make sure that she's house trained,
But that may take a while,
She is nae very happy now,
I'll try tae make her smile.

I'm sure she will nae eat too much,
I'll feed her just ye watch,
Better hide the Rhenish mind,
And keep her off the scotch.

I'll let her sleep in my room,
I'll make sure she does nae smell,
And exercise her every day,
I'll look after her well.

I'm sure that I can train her
Not tae run away
She'll have tae learn obedience
Well, that'll be the day.

Well take her tae the kitchen lad,
I'll sit her down and vet her,
Then go and take a shower lad,
The colder lad, the better

Fair is Fair

A lean and muscled body,
Came slowly into view,
Emerging from his best white sark
I want to look at you!

Nakedness before me,
There's static in the air,
Softly spoken invite,
You too then, fair is fair.

My finger traced his shoulders,
The hairs upon his chest,
Down curves of hardened muscle,
He's undressed to impress.

A touching dance of fingertips,
Not quite daring to be bold,
We feel our way together,
Neither taking hold.

I'm lifted as if weightless,
Enfolded by his arms,
Laid gently on a bed of furs,
Defenceless to his charms,

To think it was his first time,
Not quite an hour ago,
No hurry now, we've time in spades,
He'll learn to take it slow,

Bodies joined together,
As one as sparks ignite,
Passion in extremis
All earthly bonds take flight.

What is it when I touch him?
It's different from before,
What is it when he touches me,
It's special, I am sure.

More than the feel of skin on skin
More than flesh on flesh
More than I have ever known
When two like souls enmesh

This is more than physical
More than man and wife
I know that I will sell my soul
And stay with him for life

Bad dog

Its eyes were slits of yellow
It stank of flesh and death
Its scraggy fur was matted,
Hunger on its breath.
Bad Dog

I sensed its padding gait
It's low-slung creeping prowl
I heard it gather up its strength
Heard its cohort howl
Wicked Dog

Don't show fear, face it down
Watch, it's eyes will tell,
Before it springs, you'll see it
Then guard your windpipe well
Evil Dog

Right arm wrapped in velvet
Thank God for my cloak,
Leather gloves protect my hands
I hope this wolf will choke,
Back off Dog

I heard a plaintive whimpering
I struggled and I fought,
I twisted hard it's scrawny neck,
I'd break its neck I thought,
Away Dog

Bitten and bedraggled
I found the path that led
Into the woods and safety
From that foul pit of the dead.
Dead Dog

And who would send a wolf pelt,
All the way to France
With pearls bought for a lady
McCrannoch – perchance.
Old Dog

The pearls bought for the one he loved,
To match those for her neck,
The wolf cloak for a woman,
A mark of his respect.

Dirty world of intrigue

Captain Randall serves me well
Provides what I require,
His methods unconventional
Would make old nick perspire.

In this world of intrigue,
It pays to dig the dirt,
And Black Jack has a taste for it,
He thrives on human hurt,

My lifestyle lavish luxury,
My wealth a fleeting thing
I walk a line of treachery,
Between the papists and the king

I would help young Jamie
Hold him in my palm,
Use him then, like all the rest
But Randall means him harm.

We all have dirty secrets
Mucky little facts,
The secrets of our agents live
Bring fear of rope, or axe.

Oppression is the sword we wield
Deceit our closest friend,
More faces than the town hall clock,
Our morals twist and bend.

And so, my double dealing
Let Randall win the day,
He would unleash his demons
And make Jamie Fraser pay.

And I would live another day,
My wits worn to a thread,
Careful not to cross the line,
It may cost me my head.

AND SO, TO PARIS

28

Wentworth Revisited

The finest Paris offered,
In company and food,
Dreamless sleep had come for me,
Warmth with quilts ensured.

I woke with sense of something wrong,
Terribly amiss,
Freezing cold, and he was gone,
And not just for a piss.

He stared into the darkness,
Rigid and alone,
His face the shade of marble.
And stiller than a stone.

His breath came short and gasping
Muscles tensed to snap
Sweat sprang cold upon his skin
It soaked his scar crossed back

He saw the stones of Wentworth,
The horror of that cell,
The scent of degradation,
And lavender the smell.

His eyes blind as the hunted,
Frozen in the light,
I turned him to the window,
To see the moonlit night.

Tell me Jamie, talk to me,
Tell me what you feel,
Share your burden with me,
It will help you heal,

I teased from him the horror,
Perversion at its worst,
His fate described by Randall,
In detail from the first.

How he would pass his final night,
As pleasure for a beast,
Of how his body would be used,
The noose his great release,

When at the last, his bowels clenched
And all ran down his leg,
Again, he'd feel the burning pain,
Where the beast had made him beg.

He would not let me hold him,
Alone he'd fight this ghost
He slowly willed the fear away,
He would not be its host.

Neither would he use me,
Though I would give my life,
He will not salve the demon
With the love he gives his wife.

He bids me leave him quietly,
To go back to my bed,
He will be fine, I hear him say,
He knows Jack Randall dead.

He slept there in the window seat,
Wrapped in cloak and plaid
Only a dream, I heard his words
The dream that drives him mad.

He wakes as cheerful as the dawn,
To face another day,
But there is nothing I can do
To chase that dream away.

Sleepless in Paris

Paris will nae bring me peace,
From torment in ma heid,
I should be sleeping like a babe,
I'm wide awake instead,

Claire content beside me,
Carrying my child,
Softly snores and stretches,
While my mind runs wild,

Every time I close my eyes,
I'm thrown into that hell,
Fort William or Wentworth,
I can never tell.

The feel of degradation,
The fetid smell of men,
A subtle note of lavender,
The beast is in his den.

He hunts his prey across the stones,
This hound won't lose its track,
Will bring you down with fetters
And a lash across yer back.

Paralysing terror,
Muscles taught with pain,
A demon who enjoys his work,
His voice drips with disdain,

Cold hard stone, rough blanket,
The remnants of my pride,
Stripped and broken on the floor,
His will won't be denied.

And yes, I've seen men hangit!
I've seen them do deaths dance,
I knew just what dawn held for me,
I saw no worse in France.

The beast would take his pleasure,
He would make me beg,
His essence mixed with excrement,
As shit ran down my leg,

The last thing I would see in death
His face imposed on mine,
The last thing that I heard I thought,
The bellowing of kine.

That night upon MacCrannochs hearth,
He said the man was dead,
But still, I cannot find a peace,
He still invades my head.

For now, I'll find another place,
I can'nae share a bed,
Best I spend the night alone,
walk the floor instead.

I will not use ye badly,
That would not be right,
I love ye more than life itself,
And this is not your fight.

Sleep and leave me to myself,
To rid my mind of Jack,
There is no way to ease my mind,
So, sleep now Sassenach.

Dark Corners

Did he steal my soul! I think not,
Black bastard of the night,
Sassenach he showed me things
I could'na feel were right,

That pain could heighten feeling,
Make pleasure more intense,
I'd make ye beg for mercy
But it makes no sense,

That I should want tae hurt ye,
Makes me cringe in shame,
Protect ye – yes and cherish ye
Feed your burning flame,

But then I would possess ye,
Mark yer very skin,
Ride ye hard, to breaking point,
Never giving in.

Do you not think I'd do the same?
You think I'd not fight back,
Rake your skin until it bleeds,
I have a side that's black.

Bite you 'til I taste your blood,
Tease your manhood proud
I've taken you that far before,
Made you cry out loud.

I'd also hold you like a child,
Close against my breast,
Let you sleep and watch you smile,
My head upon your chest,

I love you more than ever now
For each and every flaw,
I know you love my faults as well
Deeper than before

We are two, yet we are one,
There is no other love
One inside the other,
We fit like hand in glove

Honeypot

matters of the boudoir
Are private, it's assumed,
It's where Parisian ladies
Are personally groomed.

Waxed and oiled and pampered,
Smelling at their best,
Bathed and trimmed like poodles
From their toenails to their chest.

Feeling very feminine
Devoid of all my fur,
Scented like a hyacinth
Would I his wrath incur.

First, he started sneezing,
As the fragrance hit his nose
Olfactory disturbance
likely to explode.

He likes the smell of female musk
Not flowers, they're for bees
And as for oil of hyacinth
That just makes him sneeze

Hot wax in yer oxters!
Red eyebrows disappeared,
And on yer legs as well ye say,
Where else has it been smeared,

He prowled like a stalking cat
Looking for the cream,
Just outside of scenting range
His nostrils puffing steam.

Offending scent Is washed away
To ease his nasal stress
While he calls on a roll of saints,
And watches me undress,

I haven't braved the final act,
My blushes have been saved
I haven't waxed my honeypot
He'd find that quite depraved

Bare

What do all you ladies do
When us men are at work,
Ye drink and titivate yersels
The gossip goes berserk

Sassenach yer oxters,
They are devoid of hair,
Nothing there for me tae sniff,
I love yer scent just there,

Hot wax ye say, sounds painful
Yes, stick it on yer skin,
Does it not tend tae make ye yelp?
Still, better out than in!

And yer legs, what's wrong with hair,
'Tis nature in her form
Look at mine, they've still got fur!
Just tae keep them warm,

Different it maybe,
erotic I'm in doubt
I love yer when yer animal,
A vixen, hear me out!

I din'nae need encouragement,
Tae sniff my way around,
Run my tongue up skin this smooth,
There's sweetness to be found,

Lie still there now Sassenach
I'm following ma nose,
Oh my god, yer honeypot,
Ye hid this neath yer clothes,

Best ye squeak, and squeal a bit,
I've just a breath tae catch,
'Tis far more complicated
When ye take away the thatch.

Every home should have one!

Every home should have one
Light on his feet and stealthy
Unwashed half-starved urchin
Who lives among the wealthy,

Born into a brothel
A product of his times
Stealing for a living,
The least of all his crimes.

Hands as swift as quicksilver,
A touch light as a feather
Deft and silent as a wraith
Will you feel him – never!

Bath and bed and feed him,
An asset to be sure,
Fergus is a manly name,
Not Claudel anymore.

Every home should have one,
Recruited to the cause
Charming little flatterer,
His manners taught by whores.

He grows on you like ivy
Adopted to our Clan
Stealing letters is the job
Fergus is the man.

Every home should have one,
Adopted as a son
Milord this, Milady that
wee Fergus is nae done

A child who has seen far too much
With not the best of starts
Fergus Claudel Fraser
Pickpocket of hearts

Master of Mushrooms

Milady, you have no idea
I saw the life they lead
Seen as freaks of nature
Thought the devils seed,

You say we can protect him,
He is part of our hive,
What happens though when we are gone,
How will he survive,

I tell you now of Paris,
Before I met Milord,
The morels and the Chanterelles
Abused for bed and board,

A sexual perversion,
An oddity for hire,
Valued only for their flesh,
Sold for man's desire

I had a friend amongst them,
Until I found him slain
Discarded with his throat cut,
In a sewage filled back lane,

The madame took his body,
Luc has no final rest
His organs sold in pickle jars,
To be a source of jest.

My son can have no future,
In a superstitious land
How can I protect him?
When I only have one hand.

I fear for him Milady,
What work can he do
We are as useless as each other
And you must see it too

Regrets

I didn't see this coming,
She thinks I did not care,
Greatest of all my regrets
Is that I was not there,

Now I see I was a fool,
I nearly lost it all
I was not there to hold them
I would not hear the call

I never saw her tiny hands
The wisps of bright red hair
Penitent I start each day
Because I was not there,

Forgive my sin of absence,
My anger made me blind
I was not there, I could not see
The pain I left behind.

One man's death meant more to me
I broke my oath to Claire
She asked for understanding
Again, I was not there.

I carry Faith inside me,
She's with me every day,
In a corner of my soul
Embedded there to stay

Hildegard ye named her well
Twas Faith that healed our life
Faith in name and Faith in God
And forgiveness from my wife.

BACK IN SCOTLAND

Uncle Jamie.

Me and Jenny watched you,
None of us could sleep.
I missed your warmth beside me,
Only Ian slumbered deep.

Wrapped up snuggly in your plaid,
With Kitty in your arms,
Whispering in Gaelic,
Gentle night-time charms.

You should have been a father,
When we returned from France,
But fate and my biology,
Robbed you of the chance,

Looking on the two of you,
So peaceful by the fire,
I wonder what you'll tell her,
To what she must aspire,

It must be only good things,
She's peaceful and asleep,
Safe in Uncle Jamie's arms,
While his watch he'll keep.

I still don't have much Gaelic,
But Its lilt is filled with love,
We feel like two Intruders,
Watching from above.

I have seen a part of you,
You never showed to me.
You would have done in Paris,
But that was not to be!

Taking Aim

A sample was demanded,
She would nae have refusal,
Fill this, and then bring it back,
Just for her perusal.

I have bin trampled many times,
Of mirth it's been a source,
But there's a hoof mark on ma back
Made by a British horse!

A certain camaraderie
Amongst the wounded men,
Bets are taken, wagers made.
Am I accurate ye ken.

We Scot's had won the fighting,
The British bore the scar,
But could I win their money,
By pissing in the jar.

In jest I check under my kilt,
To a raucous British cheer
Checking my equipment,
Yes, it's all still here!

I concentrate and take my aim,
Building up the pressure,
The British soldiers jeering,
Am I up to the measure?

The jar is placed, the distance marked
And as I start tae pee,
In dulcet tones I hear my Prince,
Well done, James, Mark Me!

The Devil makes a deal

Sombre clothed, in grey and black
In the shadows hid,
Grabbed my arm in vice like grip
Til I'd do what he bid

Walk with him, he meant no harm,
But talk somewhere discreet,
A proposal not for broadcast
Or discussion on the street,

Treatment for his brother,
To ease his final days,
He'd give me information,
That is how he pays.

A deal done with the devil
No one could ever know,
Black Jacks betrayal of his rank,
His brother dying – slow.

Numbers and positions,
Movements and supplies,
Intelligence for Jacobites,
Most valuable of spies.

Alex lay there wasted,
His heart and lungs so weak,
With Mary crying by his side,
He future laid out – bleak.

The last produced a prayer book,
Jack would have a wife,
At least until Culloden,
For there he'd end his life.

And Mary's child would follow,
The ancestor of Frank,
But Black Jack not his father,
He's Alex here to thank.

Did Frank find that marriage,
Know how is came to be
Did he know the witnesses?
We're Jamie – yes – and me!

Jamie damned all Randall's,
For their ghosts live in his head,
I am his and he resents
Those Randalls who aren't dead.

Franks birth is safe in history,
And I am safe in bed,
With Jamie's deepest thoughts of love,
In dreams inside my head.

He will not tell me waking,
The things he thinks in love,
He'll pass them to me in my sleep,
Where souls are hand in glove.

Jamie's Prayer

God shield her and the one she bears,
Keep them both from harm,
Lord watch over all she does,
Be her guiding arm
Keep her safe and hold her
All her journeys through,
My white dove, my brown-haired lass
I leave her care with you.
I can only watch her
Call her through the years,
You can see her safely
Through her many tears
Grant her sleep,
Grant her peace,
Grant her ease of mind,
Hold her close when I cannot,
Be the tie that binds,
bound in love before you
In doctrine and in oath,
Lord keep her and my child safe
In faith I send you both.

Flowers on the Moor

Faces to the sunlight
No pillow neath their head
Feet now rooted in the soil
The earth is now their bed

Cheering crowd of welcome
Their coloured banners wave,
When winter comes,
The cold will drive them back into the grave

Now they sing their summer song
Loud for all to see
Nature showing off her gifts,
Her show, is it free?

The bones that lie deep in the earth
That gave their mortal lives
Now feed the flowers with their flesh
In them their souls survive.

Coloured like the tartan charge
Cut down on the moor
They will blossom in the sunshine
Their memory will endure

Hidden in the winter
Like Clansmen in the heather
Plaids of earth their bodies hide
To wait for better weather.

Their seeds will spread around the world
Scattered they endure
They live in clumps still flowering
In fertile soil for sure

This multi coloured army
The soldiers of the free
Will raise its head to greet the sun
Not winter's tyranny

For now, they wave their banners
They cheer before they fight
The harsher times when flowers are dead
And all men must unite.

Dean Jackson

Dress up in your best my dear,
Like a stick if candy floss
Sit there like a lost spare part,
While Frank crawls round the boss

Don't voice an opinion,
Or pretend to have a brain,
Drink your tea politely
And from politics refrain.

A drawl that dripped with sarcasm
Dean Jackson patronised,
Held every view that I opposed,
A man that I despised.

Like an errant puppy,
I'm patted on the head,
My patriotic duty done,
In wartime and in bed.

Enjoy a life of married bliss,
Domestic servitude,
I won't submit to that with ease,
Go hang your platitudes

I hear a voice in birdsong
I feel him through the air,
His child will have a better life,
For this the cross I'll bear.

I'm not the shy retiring type,
I will not be told
What to think and what to say,
His views just leave me cold

The Dean can voice opinions
From his massive frontal lobe,
But the history professor's wife
Will always read The Globe!

Discrimination

Fellows in adversity,
Breaking down the doors,
Pushing through the barriers
Of fifties social mores

Viewed as social oddities
Expected then fail
How dare we walk these hallowed halls
We are not white and male

The black man and the woman,
Who took the class by storm.
Joe and Claire inseparable
A lasting friendship forms.

Uncle Joe is always there,
A steadfast watchful eye,
He sees it all, and nothing says
He knows her life a lie.

Go and find him Lady Jane,
There's sparkle in your eyes,
I can see you've got a man
Your glass face never lies

Am I still attractive Joe,
Tell me what you see?
Skinny broad, big hair, nice arse
You look okay to me!

Must be Brianna's father,
She's really none of Frank
A big red headed Scotsman
She has his genes to thank.

Go find him, I will steer the ship
Go find the love you crave
Go and seize your happiness,
Go, you must be brave

Lifelong friends are hard to find
Sadly, that's a fact
Like Joe and Claire forever
Opposites attract.

MEANWHILE 200YRS
BACK IN TIME

Loneliness of men

How can a soul be lonely?
In a cell with fifty men,
Human presence always there,
But no company ye ken,

By day there is unending toil,
The hunger and the cold,
By night the fruitless search for sleep,
The snores and grunts and groans,

Sometimes a little comfort,
A letter shared from home,
A tale told in the darkness,
The moonlight through the gloom.

Fights break out o'er nothing,
Man reaches out for man,
Seeking out some comfort,
They will find it where they can,

Those nights I lay there so alone,
If sleep would only come,
Then I could call you to my dreams,
Again, we could be one.

No other man would touch me,
'Ye see, you recollect
I was McDubh, I was their Chief,
They had too much respect.

Sometimes lying like a dog,
Twitching in my dreams,
Craving for a hand to touch,
Heart bursting at the seams,

Sassenach you feel my dreams,
You understand them plain
I sleep well with you by my side,
Not lonely or in pain.

Let me hold you through my darkness,
Where my demons still survive,
Your touch can drive them from my mind,
And make me feel alive.

The vision of the sacred heart,
In Paris came to mind,
The loneliness of Jesus,
Reaching out to all mankind

Parole

I could nae see his purpose,
That day we left Ardsmuir,
Taken from my kinsmen
He'd plans for me for sure,

The British will na free me but,
He keeps me close at hand,
Not banished across an ocean
To a foreign land

So where are we going,
The wee man loves tae talk,
I'm not disposed tae listen,
While the bastard makes me walk.

Indenture is but slavery
In another name,
My kinsmen sold tae bondage
Must I expect the same.

Parole is chains of honour,
Bound here by my word,
But working as a servant
To a wealthy English Lord.

'Helwater, is a fine estate,
You'll find they treat you well,'
In my mind all I can hear
Is emphasis on Hell!

'Better if you change your name,'
Which one shall I use?
I've five that I can play with,
Which one should I choose?

My body aches from walking
My mind is wracked with pain,
For those they shipped across the sea
I'll not see them again

I'm fed and clothed, I earn a wage
I should be content,
Keep my head down, shovel shit
Until my time is spent.

Finer stock I never saw,
Bloodlines to be proud,
Horses bred with quality
To stand out from the crowd.

Fresh air, hills, and horses,
Is the best that he could find
I feel a calm returning,
To the chaos of my mind

Here I'll see my time out,
Until they set me free,
Freedom is a dirty word
Who knows when it will be?

His Lordship visits monthly,
For his game of chess,
He's really looking at my arse,
I'd not expected less.

The seasons pass and all is calm,
Parole my only bond
And then here comes Geneva,
Tae cause ripples on my pond!

Ulterior Motives

We marched his kinsmen to the docks
Shipped them o'er the waves,
Seven years indenture,
They'd just as well be slaves.

Why did I not send him?
He has no further use,
The Crown will not yet pardon him
Nor send him to the noose,

A man of magnetism and fire,
He draws me like no other,
He'd kill me if I touch him so
He will never be my lover,

A friendship in adversity,
Relief from both our pain!
Conversation on a scale
To exercise the brain.

To hear him talk of things he loves,
The passion in his voice,
Educated, eloquent
A traitor not by choice.

'Twas nought to do with Frenchman's gold,
That secret is well kept,
Twas for the times I felt his pain
As silently he wept.

He is a man of honour,
And he will have his use,
If not to me then to his land
When they turn him loose.

Art, thou fallen out of heaven
Bronze statue of the dawn
I keep you close just to admire,
Lost soul of the morn.

Death and Dishonour

Ye talk tae me of honour!
De ye think me unaware
My men were banished overseas
Yet you kept me here.

Every day in servitude
Every day paroled
Robs me of my honour,
And the freedom I should hold.

Ye kept me here for reasons
I din'nae ken them yet,
I pray tae God it is nae
That ye keep me as yer pet,

Each day I wake I see them,
As you sent them overseas,
My kinsmen and my clansmen
Removed them far from me.

Dead comrades that won't see the dawn
By battle or the noose,
They have honour, I have none
Unless ye turn me loose.

Death is not romantic,
Life becomes a habit,
And I could rob ye now of yours,
As swiftly as this rabbit.

The remnants of my honour,
Will hold me as they must,
I will not allow my body,
To slake unnatural lust.

I felt it's whisper through the air
The huge fist missed its mark,
With anger born from years of loss,
He walked into the dark!

What killed the Cat

Curiosity of the Cat
Its tails leapt 'cross my skin,
Sharp the sting of leather,
Sharper than a pin.

Curiosity in two minds
How the lash would feel,
Roused a memory deeply hid,
Of wounds I tried to heal

I dreamed that night of Ardsmuir
A warped and twisted dream
A flogging engineered by one
Who would not deign to scream.

Face down and exhausted
Skin cut to the bone,
Laid out there in front of me
The two of us alone,

I dried his hair, I salved his wounds
My hands ran down his back
Naked and astride him
His façade did not crack,

Body heat between us,
And medicated grease,
Face down, laid there before me
This dreaming would not cease.

Grease, and blood, flesh, and rain,
Shame mixed in with seed.
The tears that washed my pillow
Were mine, in shame indeed.

Jamie Frasers guide to Prisons

Fort William is local,
Escape is not too hard,
The whipping post is well used
And convenient in the yard,

The food dry bread and water,
The company is poor,
Chickens are much better,
And I'm used to them for sure.

Wentworth is a doozy,
Tis fifty to a cell,
If ye get a dungeon
Then they torture ye as well,

There's hangings every morning,
Ye'll not escape the noose,
Ye don't get out of here alive,
Ye will not be turned loose.

But find the postern entrance,
Unlocked if time allows,
Ye may escape under the guise
Of fifteen highland cows.

The Bastille is a fortress,
It is nae very clean
And whilst it's French they din'nae serve
The very best cuisine

Ardsmuir was the bleakest,
The rats were at their best,
They kept me there in fetters
In case I caused unrest

The Governor could do nothing
Without I had my say,
A Masonic lodge in Prison,
Would keep disputes at bay.

Helwater was nae prison,
Twas service on parole,
Fresh air, horses, greenery
It helped tae keep me whole.

And now I'm far from Scotland
In a land they say is free,
But my wife has found a prison,
Will she stay there? Wait and see!

Guilty secrets - The upper hand

All will keep their silence
All who know the truth,
Our mother, and our father,
Who sold away her youth.

Old Ellesmere gave her status,
Though he had no charm
The young and pretty trophy wife,
Paraded on his arm

An unconsummated marriage,
Yet she was with child,
His rage was understandable
His virgin was defiled.

The heir to all his worldly goods,
Is nothing of his blood,
He'd surely take Dunsany's name
And drag it through the mud.

My brave and headstrong sister,
Told me as she died,
Just one night you lay with her,
Before she was a bride.

She loved you, so she told me,
You could not love her back,
The secret safe within these walls,
You are a father – Mac.

A broken-hearted sister,
Parents wracked with grief,
At least there is the baby,
He is their relief.

All of Ellesmere's money
Is landed with this son
He must never know his father,
You must soon be gone.

All families have secrets
Buried in the tomb
Ours is out there walking round
The image of a groom.

She told me you were kind to her,
Made her feel alive
She took that memory to her grave,
The child you gave survives

My father sold her body,
She would not sell her soul
She'd make this bargain on her terms,
And you would keep her whole.

Something to remember,
Something to understand,
The bastard in the cradle
Was Geneva's upper hand.

Meet Marsali

Mother, Wife, Companion,
Lover, Critic, Friend,
Feisty, Smart, Unstoppable,
Faithful to the end.

Run away from Scotland
To be with who you love,
Caring, Funny, Tolerant,
But not a setting dove,

Patient! And compassionate
Daughter of a wench
Putting up with Fergus
Who is very, very French,

Raised as Jamie's daughter.
Not too fussed on Claire,
But loves her as a mother
Now that Laoghaire is not there.

The Grimoire and the Ghost.

A battered notebook bound in green
Abandoned at that site
Its owner gone into the past,
And murder done that night,

Research aye and ravings
The theory of a loon,
Committed here to paper,
No familiar or broom

'It is a witches name I take,
No matter of my own,
I seek only the power of flesh,
But surrender not my bone.

Death is for surrendered souls,
I seek power absolute,
I find it makes the mind corrupt,
While I am more astute.

I study those who tried before,
No sacrifice they send
Bodies weakened by the force,
They meet a grisly end.

Samhain is the first of feasts,
When souls of heroes rise,
Those born when the stars aligned
Have power as their prize.

Few will find the courage
To use that gifted night
To leave the grave and walk abroad,
To seek what is their right.

To build an image from the stars
To walk where few would tread
To live a life that lies between
The living and the dead.

There will be one, so prophesied
His true life yet to be,
His power incorruptible
will help to set us free

He seeks one who will travel
A soul brave as his own,
One born of the auld ones
With power of her own.

And if we fail as history says,
As prophesied by seers,
The child born of this true line,
Will cross two hundred years.

Through a Spy Glass – darkly

Just to get it over with,
He'd promised her the earth,
To keep her in a lifestyle,
Far above her birth.

Where would we find the money,
We two don't have a bean,
The clothes that we stand up in,
I don't want to seem mean.

His pride won't let him give her less,
He will not do her harm,
Does not want her punished,
For the gun shot to his arm.

We stand upon a cliff top
His glass turned out to sea,
While Ian swims out to the rock,
To fetch what there might be.

A box of hidden treasure,
Put there by a witch,
Who will return to find it,
Will it make us rich?

Coincidence or destiny
Bad luck, or hand of fate
She chose to reclaim what was hers,
On this specific date.

We watch the tall ship sail away,
With Ian in its hold,
His nephew worth all life to us
So much more than gold.

Now we must leave Scotland,
Jamie won't find rest,
Until his youngest nephew,
Is returned to Jenny's nest.

Where will this journey take us?
What does fate have planned,
Now we must brave the oceans
And who knows where we will land.

He knows we go together
I've sworn I'll never leave,
I've left for good my other life
For it I must not grieve!

My vase is full of memories,
And secrets, one or two,
But never lies between us
That would never do,

A brittle trust, to share it all,
Though it will cause us pain,
Learning to know each other,
With no need to explain.

Should my heart be broken?
Should life rip us in two
You'll find my life in memories,
Held in a vase of blue.

And when life ends in mortal time,
When both our souls are free,
Bury the vase in sacred earth
With my true love next to me

OFF TO THE COLONIES

Sea Sickness

A wilted heap of blankets,
Heaped upon the bed,
The green tinged groaning monster,
Could hardly raise its head.

Go away, the only words,
To anyone who asked,
The straining, heaving reflex
Barely even masked.

Nothing stayed inside him,
His stomached had rebelled,
The sight of sour pickles,
Its wrath would not be quelled.

Try the Chinese remedy
We heard the same reply
The pair of you should go away,
Leave me here to die

Vomiting will burn your throat,
Put your insides through the mangle
Will tear your inner muscles
cause your testicles to tangle

Should that last thing happen
There only is one cure,
I would have to cut them off,
Of that You can be sure

From deep under the blankets,
A leg emerging first,
Stick me with yer golden pins!
Willoughby do yer worst,

I'll have tae trust ye Sassenach
For my balls I'll not be grieving,
And Willoughby goes o'er the side
If this does nae stop the heaving

A verra bad sailor

With eyes on the horizon
I try and hold my thoughts
The wooden deck below my feet,
A coffin lid of sorts,

The endless bobbing up and down,
Is churning up my wame,
I'd rather die than be here
If that's all the same.

Turning green around the gills,
Is not good for my pride,
I feel my breakfast rising,
Must it leap out o'er over the side,

Lying down or standing up,
Above deck or below,
I can'nae stop from puking,
Is there nowhere else tae go.

Living with a bucket
Fast between yer feet,
Three months with no solid ground,
Is really quite a feat.

Or I must suffer needles,
Poked into my head,
Looking like a porcupine,
Or taking to my bed.

Those little golden needles,
Surely do their work,
Even if the look of them
Makes me feel a burke,

Sassenach I am all yours,
Take me – do your worst,
But stop the world from spinning,
And the deck from plunging first.

Stick me with yer golden pins,
Feed me with yer tea,
And swear this is the last time,
I shall ever cross the sea.

Bolt the Door

Fevered drunk and horny,
Best describes the scene,
My Captain making light of it,
He tries to keep it clean,

Cramped up in the cabin,
No room to swing a cat,
There are somethings I'd rather swing,
I'm very sure of that.

Too weak to wield a needle
I can't inject my bum
My Captain is quite squeamish,
With the plunger 'neath his thumb.

Hotter than the fires of hell,
My skin aflame to touch,
Light of head, and addled mind,
He's not expecting much.

I will possess his body,
I know he will come round,
This fevered witch will have her way,
And never make a sound.

My mind surveys the table,
Or should we use the floor,
In between the furniture,
Different for sure.

Heavy on the Sherry,
It has the right effect,
A steaming aphrodisiac,
And I will not object.

Turtle soup, delicious
I could eat some more
Then I'll tell the captain,
He'd better bolt the door.

The Devils Arse

What is that strange thing Auntie
He chased it through the grass
Twas black and white and feisty
And stinks like the devils' arse,

I'm glad he did nae catch it,
Or at least he let it go,
It's bad enough he smells so bad
I'm sorry Auntie Jo.

Uncle Jamie where's yer gun,
We need tae shoot this beast
I'll never get the scent out,
It needs tae be deceased!

Best we move ourselves outside
Breakfast in the air,
And Ian go and bathe that dog,
I think that's only fair.

See John Quincy Myers
He'll tell ye what ye need,
Soak your hound in vinegar
Of stench he will be freed

Will ye all stop laughing
I'd swear ye all are drunk
Rollo that's the last time
Ye'll be tanglin' wi' a skunk!

Mother Claire

We've come a long way mother Claire
Since that awful day,
When ma shot da in jealous rage
Tae make ye go away,

I hated you for ages
For taking da away,
Mother said you haunted them
She could'na make him stay.

I see just how he loves ye,
That love went on and on
Surviving all the hardships
In the years that you were gone

Mother told us ye were evil
Said ye were a witch,
Wished ye dead at every turn,
She really loved to bitch.

Fergus keeps me pregnant,
I've bairns and some tae spare,
And when the next one comes along
I ken you will be there.

I love ye like a mother,
Trust ye with my life,
And as for da, my mother knew
Ye'd always be his wife.

Mrs Silversmith

I'm lookin' for the silversmith
Say lass is he by?
Nae but ye can stay and wait,
And would ye like some pie?

How long is he gone from home?
I have nae time tae bide,
I'm happy waitin' on the door
I will nae step inside,

He'll not be home for several days,
I fear your wait is long,
I'm a good cook and I've plenty,
And going for a song!

I'll take my leave, and business
Forbye, I have a wife,
If I sampled what yer cooking,
I'd be paying wi my life,

I have a bonnie cook at home,
I will nae have her vexed,
Good day tae ye Mrs Silversmith
I'll try the Blacksmith next!

Mistaken identity

Hush yer noise, sit down quiet,
I think I'll have a dram,
Rest my bones before the fire,
Shout up for yer mam.

Tonight, ye Da is in the chair
A story he must tell,
A journey with the Mohawk,
That did'na end up well,

Tell it well now Roger Mac,
Ye've an audience in awe
Maybe leaving out the bit,
Where I broke yer jaw!

Yer ma Bree was a headstrong Lass,
She left me in the mire,
She travelled off to find her Ma and Da
And warn them of a fire,

I followed her and found her,
We quarrelled and I left,
I couldn't bear to sail away,
My heart was broke – bereft.

So, I walked to Frasers ridge,
To find my handfast wife,
Yer Grand Da wasn't happy,
He nearly took my life.

Then yer uncle Ian,
sold me to a tribe,
a gang of passing Mohawk
I think they took a bribe,

They made me walk a long way north,
Tied up as a slave,
There was no way I could escape,
I'd just as well behave.

My Indian name was Dog Face,
Because of my great beard,
Indians do not have such things,
I think they thought it weird.

Yer Ma – she made them rescue me,
Yer Grand Da brought me back,
Yer Uncle Ian was the price,
Man for a man the craic!

Confusion in identity,
They thought me Stephen Bonnet,
A robber and a bad man,
I'm just Roger and I'm honest!

I got the chance to punch him back
That fiend you call Grand Da,
His heid is like an iron pot,
I didn't punch him far.

But that was all in time gone by,
We're family, and kin,
The wounds are healed over,
I have forgiven him.

Now you band of heathens,
Before ye go tae bed,
Take one lesson up those stairs,
Hold it in yer heid.

Ye Da was a professor,
in another time
Evidence and research
My tools to fight a crime.

Think before your actions
Make sure you've got the facts,
Don't go jumping in feet first,
Tis fools that do those acts.

Before you draw yer sword or dirk,
Before you throw your punches,
Make sure you've found the right boy,
Who was pulling Mandy's bunches.

Now go to bed and quickly,
The time is getting late,
Me and Grand Da need a dram,
Just to wipe the slate!

I expect your Granny's listening,
For the glasses clink,
Her broomstick's in the kitchen,
She'll be here in a wink.

Less of that now Roger Mac,
Do I have to tell you twice?
Or I shall tell the story
Of the time you lads got lice!!

Father Ferigault

He could not see his faith that way
He only saw Gods wrath
Not just the doctrine of the church,
The dogma of the cloth

Sin had tainted holy vows,
Made him fall from grace,
To fall in love and sire a child,
Had turned him from Gods face

He would not lie and bless the child
Abuse the sacrament.
To damn his child's eternal soul
he would know what was meant.

He could have stopped the torture
He had nothing to gain,
The racking screams the stench of flesh
The never-ending pain,

Baptise the child, Tis only words,
Don't let this be your hell
It's all they want, you are of faith
No matter if you fell,

All seeing lord forgive this man,
Who'd burn upon a pyre,
Take his screams up with his pain,
His faith we must admire,

They would not know the difference,
He could have been kept whole,
he knew he had betrayed his faith,
And his immortal soul,

Foolish father Ferigault,
Or one we should admire,
To make the final sacrifice
And burn in deathly fire

Warlike men who live by blood,
Will not give you release
Slowly they will turn the screw,
Your pain will never cease

That one belief should come to this
Barbaric, tortured death
His faith so strong, all pain defied
A scream his final breath.

They lit the fire beneath his feet,
Slowly stoked the flame,
Creeping heat would sear his flesh,
And then his body claim

Think of yourself, of number one,
I fled into the trees,
Escape was mine, but pain was his
It brought me to my knees.

I walked and thought, I heard his screams,
I argued with myself,
He made his choice, and he chose death
Why then should I help,

Had I lost humanity,
could I not speed his way?
The Mohawk watched inscrutable
As life was burned away.

A cask of whisky, lay at hand,
At least I'd speed his slaughter,
Pillar of fire lit up the sky,
Exploding fire water.

She placed the baby on the ground
And walked into the flame,
Their bodies moulded in that heat
Together in his shame.

Intervention

Some bright spark suggested it
A proposal soon was made,
Young Ian dressed up in his best,
His hair with bear grease laid

The answer was emphatic,
The argument began
Fraser versus Fraser,
Woman versus Man

He criticised her morals,
Her knowledge of the time,
The finger pointing gossips,
That Unwed is a crime.

The child would be a bastard,
Best ye stop and think,
He'd live his life with stigma,
Would ye no wipe out that stink.

He listed men he'd thought of,
He'd tried to find a match,
But none he ken't were suitable,
His daughter was a catch.

Ian has a tract of land,
And he'll inherit mine
Marry him I'm tellin ye
All will then be fine.

They stormed off to the stables,
Two ginger cats at war,
All flashing eyes and waving tails
I'd seen it all before.

Nose to nose they argued,
She would not give an inch,
The spitting and the hissing
Would make a tiger flinch.

Auntie leave them to it,
Best not intervene,
Two Frasers with the dander up
Are something tae be seen

Once they've traded insults
And let out all the steam
One will come out victor
The cat that got the cream

He rode off down the mountain
She stormed out of the house
Making growling noises
Like a cat plays with a mouse.

He'd cursed her in the Gaelic!
I knew it was obscene,
I'm not answering her question
What does Nighean da Ghallah mean

They'll both return for supper,
For apologies and eggs,
They may diffuse by bedtime,
But a Fraser never begs!

Termination

An inventory of poisons,
Take note of those that kill
Should I as a mother,
Offer her my skill.

Or other intervention,
My blades are whetted well,
Either way could kill her,
And the child as well.

In the slums of Paris
The Angel Makers wept
Poor unwanted unloved souls,
Smothered as they slept.

Bree does not belong here,
She wants to travel back,
The child is one more burden
That makes her outlook black,

Yet again he reads my face,
He knows what's in my mind,
Rigid now with anger,
It makes his logic blind.

Life to him is all life,
the child is of his blood
He cannot countenance the act
His words come in a flood.

To him it doesn't matter
How it came to be,
The child is flesh, his bone, his kin
He does not think of Bree!

Can he not see her trauma?
She cannot escape,
The thing that grows inside her
The product of a rape.

It's not a thing I've done before,
I'm sworn to protect life,
Instinctively he knows this,
The man can read his wife.

Him desperate for a grandchild,
Does the mother have no voice?
When all is said, and anger done
It is Brianna's choice

Return of the Mac

I'm not known as a vengeful man
Or even one of temper,
But by the time I reached the ridge,
DogFace sure had distemper.

We'd left the Mohawk weeks ago,
I'd had some time tae think,
Would I go back, just wash my hands
Well, I was on the brink.

My modern body didn't cope
With old time deprivation,
Could I ever live to see
The birth of a new nation.

This man Brianna's father
Is something to behold,
Not exactly welcoming
Her husband to the fold.

But I could'na leave her,
Not now I'd come this far
I'd have to pin my colours
To the Fraser star.

I'd never seen such hatred
The bastard could not see
Through his mist of anger,
I love his daughter Bree.

I swung a fist, I punched him,
He rubbed his iron jaw,
Raised an eyebrow thoughtfully
Then let me swing some more.

He let me punch him senseless
As he had beaten me,
Well not quite just that badly,
But I got my blows for free.

I vented all my feelings,
I think I made my point,
My last blow bent him into two
my knuckles out of joint.

We eyed each other satisfied,
He'll not think me a ponce,
But that's the last blow I would strike,
And not get a response!

The Astrolabe - A rare gift

The pedlar left his donkey
Grazing in the yard,
Handed me the parcel,
Red and breathing hard.

A box wrapped up in oilcloth,
Tied around with twine,
The seal long gone in transit,
It smelled of tar and brine.

It sat' til after dinner
Like an unexploded bomb,
Waiting to announce itself,
And do it with aplomb

Wrapped in scarlet velvet
Encased inside a box
An instrument of beauty,
It's golden finish shocks!

Eyes live with amusement
Amongst the puzzled crowd
What is it? Was the question.
The answer given, proud

Tis the planispheric astrolabe,
I ordered from Lord John
I did'na need a gold one
Pewter would have done.

Ye use it for surveying,
He handed it to Bree
I learned how tae use one
In Paris don't ye see

They examined the engraving,
Called extravagance a crime,
Then father took his daughter out
To learn to tell the time.

An instrument of quality,
The engraving seems alive
Align the discs and you will know
It's twenty-five past five

He stiffened as he read the note
Suffice it all to say
This instrument had not been bought
By his good friend Lord John Grey

I felt the arrow strike its mark
The barb stuck in his heart
William 9th Earl Ellesmere
In this had had his part.

Buy the finest and the best,
To him this would mean gold,
A token from a lifelong friend,
And the son he could not hold.

The Butter churn

Father Kenneth was arrested
And under some portent
Desirous of his services,
We stole into the tent

To get his grandson christened
Jamie must distract the crowd
So, he made confession
Embarrassingly loud

His lewd imagination
Had run amok it seems,
With a lassie churning butter,
Who stirred alluring dreams.

He watched her at the handle
The rhythm stirred his lust
Breasts heaving with the motion,
Pull and push and thrust,

Her skirts swayed to the movement
Her face aglow with sweat
Impure thoughts ran through his mind
And through his body swept,

He saw her pitching forwards,
Bent across the churn,
Skirts hitched high above her waist,
His ardour starts to burn,

And I outside the tent flap,
Speechless and amazed
Listened as he outlined
His intentions – quite depraved!

Described in every detail,
Every squeak she'd utter,
And everything he'd done to turn
Her insides into butter!

I remember that encounter well,
My cheeks begin to burn,
Remembering the afternoon
We broke the butter churn!

Seeing Double

When it comes to finding husbands,
Lizzie causes much ado
A quiet and hardworking lass,
You'd think there'd be a queue.

McGillivray the gunsmith,
Fiancé number one,
Slept with a whore and caught the pox,
He left town at a run!

Then Young Bobby Higgins,
Would have tried his case,
But Mr Wemyss won't entertain
That brand upon his face,

The Beardsley's her protectors
Won't see her come to harm,
There's two of them identical,
Is that cause for alarm.

For Lizzie is alas with child,
The dirty deed is done
Is it Kezzie or Josiah,
She must marry one!

All called to the 'speak a word'
Himself is in a rip,
Make an honest woman,
Or He'll sort it with a whip.

Three young minds together,
Are too much for the Laird
Married one and hand fast two
The three of them are paired.

Time is a great healer
Folk get used to much,
And Lizzie Wemyss love life
To all is double Dutch.

Mistress Forbes Picnic

Mistress will ye dine wi me?
I giggled like a child.
A courtly bow, a cheeky grin
I looked at him and smiled.

My wife has left me wanting,
She's gone off tae a birth,
I saw the sun glint off his hair,
Laughed for all I'm worth.

My! he is a handsome man,
Well mannered, so polite.
Why should I not go with him,
Would Neil not think it right.

Mistress I'd steal ye away,
To picnic 'neath a tree,
The weathers fine, as is the food,
You'll surely come wi me!

One hand on the basket,
He swept me up like dust,
Drove me in his carriage,
And over me he fussed.

I saw his blue eyes twinkle,
He flirted and he'd flatter
Courtly manners to the fore,
His words a silken patter

Why would Mr Fraser want,
A lady such as me?
I am older than the hills
Have more wrinkles than his tree

I had such fun that afternoon,
Nothing did, I fear.
But what on earth had Neil done?
That he should lose an ear.

Forbes Ear

Brianna had been taken
Held on Bonnets craft
Kidnapped by the lawyer,
Is Neil Forbes quite daft.

He sat there in the parlour
Enjoying a strong cider,
Self-satisfied, and gloating
She's where no one will find her,

A hand upon his shoulder,
Brings him back to life,
Roger Mac, a grip of iron.
Where sir is my wife.

Forbes denies all knowledge,
Rogers eyes a laser,
Ian Murray with a knife.
But where is Jamie Fraser.

Jamie is off picnicking,
He's calling on Forbes mother,
A kidnap is a grand day out,
He charms her like no other.

A messenger, a note is sent
A brooch as proof of deed,
Forbes spills all to Roger Mac,
To get his mother freed.

Bonnets ship Anemone
Set sail for English shores
Brianna as a cargo,
Along with slaves and whores.

Her father would have searched for her
Far across the seas
Forbes problem with James Fraser
Instantly would cease.

Roger springs plans a rescue
Forbes has cause to fear,
Ian's knife is swift and sure
In cutting off Forbes ear,

A talisman to find her
The Mohawk way, he grins,
And a reminder to a lawyer
Don't mess with Fraser kin!

Anaesthetics

The ability to operate
Without the patient screaming,
A body lying limp, relaxed
In a state of dreaming.

Copious quantities of drink
Will help to stay the nerves,
But it will not stop the pain,
It taxes the reserves.

Laudanum will induce a sleep,
But also brings a frown,
The patient needs restraining still,
Sometimes tying down.

The brave will suffer surgery
With a gag between their teeth,
Screaming through their rigid jaws
To find some slight relief.

The art of making ether,
Using its sweet vapour,
Will send the strongest man to sleep
But do not light a taper!

More complicated surgery
Can then be undertaken
With the patient sleeping peaceful
But please don't be mistaken

Ether is a fickle thing
Its synthesis is danger,
Alcohol and Vitriol
Are better kept as strangers,

High risk of explosion,
Greater risk of fire,
One degree on either side
Can land you in the mire.

So, I make it in the shed,
And hope that no stray spark
Blows me into smithereens,
While working in the dark.

There is one good chemist
Who makes It, unafraid,
A soldier's cure for seasickness
He sells It ready made.

Calling Roger Mac

It will turn ye off ye sandwich
A look from Old Arch Bug
His face will make the milk turn
Before it leaves the jug

A chip upon his shoulder
Like to weigh him down,
Everything a grumble
And like as not a frown.

Trouble lays on trouble,
I have nae time for lunch,
I'd find those twins and lay them out,
They're hidin I've a hunch

Ye say that in the future,
Some will not eat meat,
I ken ye don't like killin
But what then would ye eat

When I catch up with the Beardsleys
Ye ken I'll make them shiver
Would a vegetarian
Excuse me eatin' liver.

I ken ye have a calling,
I see ye care for folk
Kindness flowing in yer veins
And ye can take a joke.

Follow where yer heart leads
Where ye can do most good,
Not all men are hunters,
And they don't go short of food.

We din'nae have a minister,
We din'nae have a priest,
Tom Christies words will burn our ears
Before his chidings ceased.

Go then, make it formal
Get yerself ordained,
Then say one for the Beardsley Twins
Before they end up maimed.

Hands of time

Time stops
When I take her hand
I hold it tae my lips
My eyes hold hers
My love flows out
To her fingertips
Hands which work
Hands that heal
Hands which hold each hurt I feel
Hands which stitched
Hands which bled
Hands which guide me up tae bed

My soul leaps
When he takes my hand
His lips soft on my skin
His kiss is light like gossamer
Brushing where it's thin
Eyes locked on mine
He sees my soul
Reads my inner thoughts
Passion checked

His face reflects
As all my love he courts

Workers hands
Rough from the fields
Fingers long and deft
Explore my palms in worship
The right one
And the left.
Hands say much about a life
Tis all writ in a palm
Life and love and future
Scripted like a psalm,

Take my hand
You hold my life
My touch you understand
Linked in love my tread our path
To find out what God planned

What is Faith

It is not just observing
the ritual of the church
Faith is holding a belief,
a vision of its worth,

The ceremonial service,
The formal observation
Is there to focus all your thoughts
To aid your meditation,

A priest is but a conduit,
He helps to spread the word,
And shares the burden of your sin
With each confession heard,

Belief that there is purpose
Belief in man's endeavour
Belief in your eternal soul
Is faith you hold forever.

Faith does not need a building,
Faith does not need a priest
Faith does not need religious cant
All faith needs is belief.

Faith will guide your actions,
Faith will heal your soul
When all is lost, and hope is gone
Faith will keep you whole.

Living with a man of faith
Is difficult at times,
For he believes that one true being
Absolves him of his crimes.

His faith in his ability
To walk his chosen path,
Will surely take us journeying
A long way from our hearth.

My faith is much more simple,
I don't act on a whim,
I consider all pertinent facts,
And then have faith in him

Valentine's Day

Spring is in the mountains,
The green begins to show.
Frost still crisps my morning tread,
At least we don't have snow.

Don yer cloak and walk with me,
Breath white on the air,
See the sunrise bring the day,
Light up this country fair.

Am I enough still Sassenach,
Do I keep ye whole,
I din'nae doubt ye love me,
Tis you who guards my soul.

Let's walk in yer garden,
Through your line of hives,
Hear the bees awaken,
Their busy, buzzing lives.

Today is marked by Valentine,
Fertility and love,
We don't need gifts of flowers,
My white-haired setting dove

Nature looks best in its place,
Growing wild and free,
Or tended in a garden,
To satisfy the bee.

We don't need toys and trinkets,
We say it with our eyes,
One look from you and I am lost,
For you I'd steal the skies

Let's walk a while amongst the bees,
Update them with the news
Then up to the high ground,
Let's take in the views,

Lie like in our younger days,
When heather was our bed,
When all we had was in our bags,
And laid beneath our head.

Look out over mountains,
Endless lines of trees,
This land of opportunity,
That brought us to our knees.

I can'nae do without ye,
Tis you that keeps me strong,
The bond between us forged in time,
More than a lifetime long

In all the coming turmoil,
Should we have to part,
Remember me for ever,
Store me in your heart.

We din'nae need the trappings,
Which show the worth of life,
I like ye best in just yer skin,
My feisty English wife.

Ye never needed finery,
Ye never asked fer much,
Ye always had the power,
Tae thrill me with yer touch.

Spread yer cloak around us,
Lie here on my plaid,
My Valentine, my calman geal
Yer husband needs ye – bad

Ode to perfection

It's stopped his plaid from falling down,
For over twenty years
It fills his breeks so nicely,
When viewing from the rear

tough as saddle leather,
From sitting on his horse,
I've sat behind it many times
Nice and close of course.

Firm and pert and shapely,
Just below his back
Perfect globes encased in cloth
Like boiled eggs in a sack,

Admire from a distance,
Touch it – don't you dare,
The miracle that's Jamie's arse,
Is property of Claire!

.

Beehive Yourselves

It's all gone very quiet,
I can hear no din!
In the silence you can hear
The dropping of a pin.

Mailboxes are opened,
Deliveries are completed.
Half the world is full with Bees
The rest are feeling cheated.

Comfy seats are de-rigeure
Chores are put on hold,
Neglected husbands scratch their heads,
And do as they are told.

The longest incubation,
But now we've given birth,
To anticipated pages,
Now we'll read for all we're worth.

No bickering can follow,
For those not in the know,
This plot line weaving through the book,
Is not yet in the show.

Pages turn, eyebrows are raised,
Is this what we expected,
No spoilers yet to mar the read,
To make you feel dejected.

What is your poet doing?
While this silence is in place,
Is she sitting idly,
Staring into space.

I may have found a peaceful spot
Underneath some trees,
Where if I listen, I can hear
the buzzing of the bees.

Acknowledgments

As always, I acknowledge the amazing work of Diana Gabaldon without which this homage would not be possible.

The work of the writers, producers, actors and production crew of Starz and the Outlander Team.

I will also mention my home-grown editing team, who exist on social media and pull me up on punctuation, grammar and spelling, content, accuracy and occasionally make very pertinent suggestions. I take all your observations in good heart and will usually act on them. I do not stretch to a formal editing team: I am a one-man band on a shoestring.

I also acknowledge the artistic talents of Lyn Fuller who allows me to use her artwork for my covers.

Other Work by the Author

This book is the 10th Book in the series of
unofficial books of Outlander Inspired Poetry:

.

Unofficial Droughtlander Relief

The Droughtlanders Progress

Totally Obsessed

Fireside Stories

Je Suis Prest

Après Le Deluge

Dragonflies of Summer

Semper in Aeternum

Sia Air Ochd

The Blue Vase – in Hardback and illustrated

I hope the Princess will approve – a book of
COVID and equine related poems.

Ginger like Biscuits – the adventures of a
Welsh Mountain Pony

Rhymes and Rosettes

Pixie Saves Christmas

The author may be contacted by email:
chestyathome@aol.com
and sells through Amazon and also through
the Etsy Shop – Poemsandthings which can
supply book bundles at a discount rate

RDA

It's what you can do that counts

Riding for the Disabled Association
Incorporating Carriage Driving

Printed in Great Britain
by Amazon

83365332R00089